Lemons, Limes and Tangyryne

Written by Sharmayne A. Whyte
Illustrated by Genevieve Townsend

ISBN 978-1-989832-02-8

Story by Sharmayne A. Whyte
Edited by Jennifer Blanchard and Kameryn Whyte
Illustrations by Genevieve Townsend
Design and layout by Cameron Montgomery at Studio Dreamshare Press
Cover art by Genevieve Townsend
Headshot photography by Sharolyn Townsend Photography and Sharmayne A. Whyte

Studio Dreamshare Press
Pembroke, Ontario
www.StudioDreamsharePress.com
For information and permissions contact:
publishing@studiodreamshare.com

I dedicate this book to my three wonderful children, Michael, Phoenyx and Kameryn. Thanks so much for your support. To our dog Tangyryne, you will always be in our hearts and thank you for always being there for Kameryn.

“Mommy, what are you looking for?” I asked.
Mom was looking around the house for something.

“Why little girl Alisha,” she said kindly, “I am looking for my lemons and limes.”

“Lemons and limes?” I repeated.

“Yes,” Mommy said. “Yesterday, I went to the market and bought a dozen lemons and a dozen limes,” she explained. “I only used a few in our lemonade, but now I seem to be missing a few.”

I
Veggies
TANGERINES
$3.99 lb.

“Tangyryne and I will help you look,” I said.

Around the house my dog Tangyryne and I went, looking for lemons and limes.

We looked in the cupboards, but not a single one was there.

Bread
Butter
Berries

We looked in the kitchen and under the chairs.

We looked in the closet and didn't see a thing, not
a single lemon or lime!

When I lifted up the cushions on the couch, Tangyryne jumped up and down to look as well. I searched in the back and sides of the couch, but I did not find a lemon or a lime.

“I know,” I thought to myself, “I will check under my bed.”

So up to my room Tangyryne and I ran. We searched under my bed.

I moved my slippers and some toys, but still we could not see any lemons or limes at all.

Tangyryne and I ran back to the kitchen to see if Mommy had another clue.

“Mommy, can you show Tangyryne what a lemon and lime look like, just so she knows what she is looking for?”

FAMILY
WOW
LOVE

As soon as my mom showed Tangyryne the lemon, she grabbed it quickly and ran.

“Oh no!” I shouted as I ran after her. “Please bring the lemon back.”

Tangyryne kept running as I followed behind and I ran into her when she stopped.

Then she dropped the lemon, lifted up her bed, and tried to roll the lemon under it. As I looked at her something came to mind.

“Mom come quick!” I shouted.

Mom came to the den.

"I think I know where all your lemons and limes are going," I said.

“They are all under Tangyryne’s bed.”

As Mommy bent down and lifted Tangyryne’s bed, she saw lemons and limes galore.

I looked at Tangyryne.

“Oh silly Tangyryne. Lemons and limes are not for dogs!”

The End.

CPSIA information can be obtained
at www.ICGtesting.com
Printed in the USA
LVHW070122171121
703501LV00002B/12